Henry Holt and Company, Inc.
Publishers since 1866
115 West 18th Street
New York, New York 10011

Henry Holt is a registered trademark of Henry Holt and Company, Inc.
Text copyright © 1996 by Karen Wallace
Illustrations copyright © 1996 by Peter Melnyczuk
Published by arrangement with Hodder Children's Books
The author and/or illustrator asserts the moral right
to be identified as the author and/or illustrator of this work.
First published in the United States in 1996 by
Henry Holt and Company, Inc.
Originally published in England in 1996 by Hodder Headline

Library of Congress Catalog Card Number: 95-80434

ISBN 0-8050-4636-4
First American Edition—1996

Printed and bound by Oriental Press, Dubai
1 3 5 7 9 10 8 6 4 2

Imagine You Are a
TIGER

KAREN WALLACE

Illustrated by PETER MELNYCZUK

HENRY HOLT AND COMPANY ◆ NEW YORK

Imagine you are a tiger.

A tiny tiger is born in a den on dry grass.
His eyes are shut tight and he mews like a kitten.
He scrambles through his mother's fur and finds her milk.
The tiny tiger sucks until his belly is full.

Imagine you are a tiger.

A little tiger creeps from his den.

His eyes are open now.

He sees a green parakeet flutter from a tree.

He sees a black-faced monkey jump in the branches.

He hears quick steps behind him.
His mother is standing over him.
The stripes on her fur look like shadows on the ground.
She picks up the little tiger and holds him in her jaws.
He hangs floppy as a rag doll
as she carries him back to the den.

Imagine you are a tiger.
A young tiger grows quickly.
He wrestles with his brother.
He snarls and bares his teeth.
He pounces and pulls his brother to the ground.
Soon the young tiger will hunt in the forest.

The sun is high in the sky. The air is hot and dusty.
The young tiger follows his mother down to the river.
He watches her wallow in the water.
He sits on the shore, wanting to be with her.

A young tiger quickly learns to swim.
He leaps and splashes with his brother.

Then he lies in the shade
and watches the river through half-closed eyes.

Deer come.

They stand on flat rocks to drink in the sun.

They are frightened of the tigers.

But the flat rocks burn like oven plates.

They are too hot for tiger paws.

The deer's hooves keep them safe.

Wild boars come.

They grunt and jostle by the water.

They hide their piglets under a thorny bush.

They are frightened of the tigers.

The boars' tusks are sharp. Their skin is tough as old leather.

But their piglets are fatty and sweet.

Imagine you are a tiger.
A young tiger sees his mother steal from the water.
She leaps through the shade to the thorny bush
and snatches a piglet.

The young tiger runs with his brother after his mother,
over the grassland and into the forest.

She gives them the piglet and lies down beside them.
A hungry young tiger eats as much as he can.

Imagine you are a tiger.

A fierce, full-grown tiger strides through the long grass.

His stripes look like stalks.

His gold fur shines like sun on the ground.

He sees a deer on her own.
He crawls on his belly, ready to spring.
A black-faced monkey screams in a treetop.
The deer hears his warning and bounds away.

A cunning tiger crouches in the grass.

He waits and listens.

He hears hoofbeats thud on the hard ground.

He peers through the grass with clear yellow eyes.

An antelope is crossing the scrubland toward him.

Imagine you are a tiger.